All Blocks Gone

Proposed, edited by

Writing from the Head

All Blocks Gone

This edition published by Headway Glasgow

In association with Writing from the Head (a group within Headway Glasgow)   260 Bath Street, Glasgow G2 4JP www.headwayglasgow.org.
Copyright 2012 © 2012 Writing from the Head
 All authors maintain moral and legal rights to the undernoted works a list of whom appears on page 75. No part of it may be reprinted or produced or utilised in any form or by electronic, mechanical or other means now known or hereafter invented, including photocopying and recording or in any information storage or retrieval system without permission in writing from the individual author and their right to be identified as the author being asserted. Permission to reproduce or reprint can be obtained directly with the author or through Headway Glasgow.

ISBN - 978-0-9574693-1-0 PAPERBACK
ISBN - 978-0-9574693-0-3 E READER

A CIP catalogue record for this book is available from the British Library.

Printed by Clydeside Press, 37 High Street, Glasgow.

Every effort has been made to contact copyright holders. However the publisher will be glad to rectify in future editions any inadvertent omissions brought to their attention

Acknowledgements

The editors would like to thank the following for making sure this book was produced

All the authors and artists who contributed their work - Including ourselves.

Sean Cumming for starting us off in this direction and encouraging us to write before fleeing to China to leave us to finish the job
Annette Allison for badgering and assisting people in the Drop-in to finish their contributions
Carol Alexander for sorting out the art work so we could make a choice
The Staff at Headway Glasgow for giving their support through thick and thin
Long Term Conditions Alliance Scotland staff for putting up with us week after week.
Brainiac for believing we could keep going to the end and helping find a workspace.
Kathleen and her team at Digby Brown Solicitors for freeing up our minds to give attention to this project.
And to all the others who also helped us clear away the blocks to creativity.

Writing from the Head editorial group

Rosemary   Jim   Steven   Neill

This book was able to take shape and to be completed with the financial assistance of **Scottish Community Foundation** to whom we are very grateful

scottish
community
foundation

Headway Glasgow

Registered charity number SC030113

For more information about Writing from the Head or to purchase extra copies of this book please contact:
Headway Glasgow,
260 Bath Street,
Glasgow, G2 4JP.
Website: www.headwayglasgow.org
email: info@headwayglasgow.org

Telephone number: 0141 332 8878

To allow Headway Glasgow to continue the work we have been doing with those affected by Acquired Brain Injury, donations can be made through our website using giftaid or sent to the above address.

TO PURCHASE FURTHER COPIES PLEASE CONTACT US AT THE ABOVE ADDRESS

PREFACE

Writing from the Head is a small group consisting of people who have an Acquired Brain injury together with a volunteer. The group was formed within Headway Glasgow, a charity which deals with people who have an Acquired Brain Injury. The function of the group is to attempt to encourage members to gain confidence through discussion and writing in a self- help environment. Concentration, fatigue, being easily stressed and memory problems are just some of the issues to be faced on a daily basis. As a group we aim to help and encourage each other to be as creative as we can. Having no time limits and being surrounded by like- minded people enable us to attempt to achieve this.

The group decided to set up its own blog to act as a showcase for its activities and out of that came the idea of producing this book. It was felt that other members and volunteers in Headway Glasgow might have some writing or artwork of their own to contribute to this enterprise. After some cajoling, articles started to come in and in a very little time there were enough contributions to go ahead with the project. So with many thanks here is a list of contributors whose work is featured in the book.

Check out our blog writingfromthehead@tumblr.org.

A list of contributors follows

Rosemary Boyle, J.V, S. West, John Campbell, Leo Mushet. Mark Osborne, Vivien Paton & Tom Paton, DT, Margaret Thomson, Lorraine Kennedy, Michael Gallagher, Annette Allison, Bob Colquhoun, Innes Walker, Pandora, Stuart McIntyre, Sean Riach, Looby Loo, Jane McQueen, Neill Sloan, John Barr, Karen Mitchell, Clair Parker, Graham Harkness, Kirsty Lockhart.

Contents: Poems & Stories

Contents: Art

Poems & Stories

They are gone 1
By Margaret Thomson

They are gone
I miss them
I wasn't even aware of them
But I miss them
They are gone

They used to do things for me
And I never even knew
Everyday tasks I took for granted
But now they are gone
And oh how I miss them

They say-you don't know what you've got
until it's gone
How true – I never knew
And now I miss them
They didn't just leave
They died

They could not be revived
I never knew how I relied
Upon them
But they are gone
And I am bereaved

Each day I cry
I cry for them
For they are gone forever
And I miss them

The brain cells have died
They could not be revived
I never knew how I relied
Upon them
And now they are gone

Poem for Elizabeth
By Leo Mushet

You've always been in my life
Right from the start
Holding my hand when I got scared
Always in my heart

We played games and had our fun
You never made me cry
But something happened to my heart
The day you left my side

In my heart and in my mind
This person will be there for the rest of my life
Although you're gone I'll always feel you with me ...
...it's the way I feel inside

I try to go on living my life
but you never leave my mind
As I grew up it got too hard
And I became unkind

I know it's not what you wanted
I'm sorry I took that road
But I'm trying now to make you proud
And let the good unfold

Every time I think of you
I can't stop the tears
You're in my thoughts and in my heart
For the rest of all my years

My Favourite Place 3
By Lorraine Kennedy

I go on holiday with my mum to an old monastery up near Perth, it's not Australia but it is really relaxing. I look forward to going with my mum and my auntie every year, it's good to spend time with them.

There used to be a wee man who worked there for years but he died recently. You get to know the people, ordinary people. There are vegetables, flowers and animals; it's all nicely laid out. They have birds and a scarecrow. It's a big garden which you can walk about in.

It's a religious place. We have masses, we have talks. It's a spiritual place. There's a sitting room upstairs. You can sit and relax and read. They have two television rooms where you can sit and watch the news after you've been fed and watered. It is good food and good company. I like being there. It's nice to be away from the city, from the boring shops.

You can get into Perth town. I prefer to stay with my mum at the monastery I don't like the shops. I wouldn't like to live there permanently it'd be boring but it's nice for a change. That's my favourite holiday place. But some day I'll go to the other Perth.

4

About an Auntie
By Sean Riach

Well mannered curt curls
Ruby flashes of blue through
A grey undercurrent
Large thick specs concealing
Sharp still water Iris
A hunched figure knitted
Into her favourite chair
Where after her death
Sleepwalking I saw
Through the ridges
Of frosted glass
A bundle of tartan
Surrounded by a halo
Of unopened cake tins

Her rock cakes were literal
Hard as granite, gravel flavoured
They shaded the gums and teeth
In rich seems of charcoal.
Sponge cake would absorb
All the moisture in your mouth
The teabag on its fifth pot
Like gargling in turpentine
To my memory she is otherworldly
Pillbox fox fur hat
Electric blue fedora
With ostrich feather eye
A shrunken head in ebony

Or a backwards projection of
The stories I have inherited
Cycling across Europe
On a tandem Summer 1939
Perceptively she noticed
'Nothing out of the ordinary'

Counting rolling stock
In Nigeria in the 50's
Collecting objet d'art
From local craftsmen
Offering three week old
Cherrycake without cheer
Unaware of the disturbing
Brutishment of it all

For the Love of a Son or Daughter
By Rosemary Boyle

Wishing them happiness and contentment for the future

Hopes that they will be healthy

Looking forward to their first teeth

Awaiting with anticipation to their first steps

From an early age allowing their child to choose the clothes they wear. This helps build self-confidence in them which helps with their future.

Thinking of their first day at school.
Seeing them in your minds eye
Sitting at their tiny desk
Surrounded by their new friends.

As they progress through school,
Watching your child taking part in their first play.
Boy what a wonderful sensation of pride
Just as you had hoped.

Dreams of their future career.
Will they become a Doctor
A Nurse
A Plumber
An Electrician
or an Artist

What sports will they play? Football,
Rugby, Hockey, Badminton, Tennis
or dreams of becoming a professional
sportsperson.

When will they pass their driving test?
What will their first bike and car be?

Hopes of their child finding love
Who will your child choose?
Very often it is said
a son will choose someone with the characteristics
of his mother and a daughter will choose someone
just like her dad.

Being thankful for the love of your partner
and the love they feel for their child
and yourself.

All in all, it is a parents dream for their child to
have everything their heart desires and more, much
much more. A parent will do their utmost to see to
it that their child has a wonderful start in life. And
as they progress through the various stages of life
they will do all that they can for them and show the
love of a parent.

Travelling Light
By Looby Loo

A couple of years ago a good friend of mine asked if I would like to go a trip to Lochgilphead for the weekend.

The weather at that time was beautiful and by the time we started our trip, weather reports were uplifting. I had made up sandwiches, and had fruit, and a flask of hot water for the trip. The journey was pure magical. We arrived in Arrochar and had a wee "tea break"; the sun was shining through the trees and onto Loch Long. Absolutely beautiful! The only place I had been at in Scotland was Saltcoats, where my father took the family when we were youngsters. So this was a new experience.

We carried on round to Inveraray where there is a lot of history which I can't remember. It was just your luck if you get stuck behind a lorry or a tractor, but we got there eventually. We went into a wee shop there and it sold lots of different sweeties, i.e., MB Bars, rhubarb & rock and whoppers (if anybody remembers them) and ice cream. I had a large cone which lasted me a long time, a wee lick here and there because it tasted so amazing.

Back into the car and on our way round to
Ardrishaig where we stopped for a pub lunch, which
was lasagne, and it tantalised my taste buds with
garlic bread, washed down with blackcurrant and
lemonade.

As we travelled on to Lochgilphead we tried to
book into the caravan park but it was full so we
came to a decision to carry on into Campbeltown for
accommodation. The guy in the caravan park
phoned another caravan park to see if there were
any vacancies. The answer was yes and the place
was Machrihanish. The journey was so exciting,
scenery was fantastic, and the sun was shining from
morning till night. What else could we ask for? We
settled down for the night in our "home" and I fell
asleep thinking of the next day as my friend had told
me about the golf course at Machrihanish.
Seemingly you tee off over the Atlantic Ocean. I
thought he was "off his heid". I slept terrifically.

We got up early next morning and went into
Campbeltown for breakfast to start a new day. We
came back and Bill showed me the golf course and
he was true to his word. He took me to where the
golfers tee off and I could see what he meant.

The sea was so blue and we strolled along the
beach for a while. Later he took me a run to
Southend where we saw the seals and baby seals. I
also saw when the tide was out, a path that took you

over to caves. There's a story to that as well, again I can't remember.

Then we stopped at a spot where I had a profound spiritual experience. It was as if the sun came out just for me at that moment, it was shining so bright onto the very calm, blue sea. It was awesome. It's something that will always stick in my mind. I am so grateful my friend suggested the wee break.

Cycles
By Neill Sloan

Today it has taken me two hours to climb to the top of the hill, a journey that once would have taken me half an hour, but since my head injuries, I find that I have to take my time. That is no great loss, as now I have an excuse to take in that Nature you so often miss on the way. Young Seonaid can do it in under that time... it is a pleasure to watch. I think back to 1984 when I had my "accident" and visions of my big brother spring to mind. Then I was too busy having a good time to pay any attention to him.

Drugs and alcohol were all the rage amongst my friends and at one particular party I decided to cycle home, mostly downhill. That evening I made a detour to the Accident and Emergency via a brick wall. Strangely, I was allowed to go home, with some serious bleeding inside my skull, but they didn't know it.

About four days later my flatmates noticed that there was something not right with the "corpse" in the bedroom. I was taken to the doctors and was told I needed immediate hospitalisation. Not waiting for an ambulance the doctor drove me there in his own car. At A&E I am left with staff who ask asked me questions to which I can only moan once for yes and twice for no. In hospital you lose all sense of the real world. Outside everything is done for you or you are told when to do it. My whole way of thinking is slowed down and I couldn't be bothered with all the things needed to sustain life. I have a drip inserted into each arm. The thing I remember most is the hallucinations.

I have a sub-dural haematoma causing a build up of pressure in my brain which threatens to kill me if something is not done immediately. The surgery lasts for slightly more than two hours.

After the surgery I go to the intensive care ward. This is a scary place, no overhead lighting, no noise apart from the machines that keep the patients alive. The nurses refer to it as "death alley" due to the rapid turnaround of patients. Back in an ordinary ward once more my body starts undergoing violent seizures. I am taken back to surgery once more. This time when I return nothing seems to be working.

I woke up and I could not move the right hand side of my body. The left hand side was not there either, not even a polite "please" would make it work. Alistair my flat mate visits me every day to keep me informed as to what is happening at the farm and to bring me music. The parents arrive later. I hear that they met me as I came out from the theatre. My mother has become ward translator as there are lots of Scottish people on the ward and the nurses were having difficulties understanding them. It made me laugh to see this which was a positive after so many negative sensations that I had felt at the time.

The momentous day came when I moved my big toe on my left foot, nineteen years before a similar scene in Kill Bill. Nothing stopping me now apart from the tubes. It could be dangerous moving about but my parents were there to help me if I fell.

One day an odd piece of apparatus was wheeled up to my bed. Immediately changing it into a bus. What's this I wondered. Looked like an implement of torture which was for pull ups. Said one nurse. I couldn't lift my arms up to the bar so they had to lower the bar for me to grab. They then lifted it, but because my hands and arms were so weak they would just fall off.

Five weeks after having had two operations on my brain and a further week in hospital, I was discharged. My mates took me home to the farmhouse. For the main part I was left alone. It must be like being released from prison, to be free to get up when you want and go to bed when you feel like it.

An ambulance arrived to take me to physiotherapy, no mean feat, since the house is half a mile from the nearest paved road. Walking is hard but if I concentrate then after the first few steps it is not bad, apart from a noticeable limp. After a week of bumping down the track to collect me, the lift is cancelled, because the ambulances are breaking

14

down. I can't walk, don't have a car. The only alternative is to get on my bike. This involved three hours of active rehab, before I even get to the Centre. After two weeks of this I am now able to beat the local bus.

The chief physiotherapist finds me cycling into the centre one day. Just after mid-morning break he calls me into the office to have a 'wee word' I go in and find most of the Heads of Departments are there as well.

-Have a seat Neill. This doesn't look good

-Where have you cycled from?

-The farm

-How far is that

-It's about fifteen miles away,

-You do this twice a day, five days week?

-Yes

-How long has this been going on?

-For about four weeks, since the ambulance stopped coming for me,

-Neill, you have been cycling here thirty miles a day, five days a week for about a month! I'm afraid we are going to request that as from Monday next week you stop coming.

It's hard to write a poem
By Mike Gallagher

It's hard to write a poem
Especially one that rhymes
I know because I've tried it
Many, many times

It's hard to write a poem
The words are hard to find
I know they're hiding somewhere
Up there in my mind

It's hard to write a poem
I think I'll write a play
I've no words to write a poem
I'll try another day

A refuge
By Margaret Thomson

Where ability is not measured or mentioned

Where no judgement is passed

Where acceptance is the key

Where normal is all and all is normal

This is my refuge

This is where disability disappears

This is Headway

Going on the Steam Train
By Alexandra McQueen

My favourite childhood memories would be at my aunt's caravan up at Burntisland with my Mum, Dad, Nana, Granda, brother and sister. We used to love running barefoot in the sand, with the sun beating down on our backs. It felt as if we were abroad, it seemed as if it was sunny the whole time we were off school.

I loved going up to my Nana's when she baked her dumpling wrapped up in muslin, full of silver sixpences, waiting for it to dry in front of the fire.

My Granda cutting the grass with his old fashioned lawn mower. The sweat pouring out of him, trying to get through all the weeds. Pruning his roses, vivid red, bright pink and yellow and the smell filled the whole garden with this brilliant aroma. I like the smell of freshly cut grass. It still takes me back to my childhood.

I dance doing my housework listening to T-Rex blasting out in the background. Marc Bolan was my idol, I had his posters all over my bedroom wall, if only it was 1975 again. It takes me back to my teenage years.

My Favourite Place 1
By Bob Colquhoun

My favourite place was the BB Camp Site at Benderloch, Argyll (7 miles outside Oban). We learned to camp under canvas when I was twelve years old.

It was strange at night time when the cows in the field used to lie down beside the tents. It was the body heat that attracted them to the side of the tents.

We obtained drinking water from an overflow which went into a stream. Daily we would take 1 gallon or 5 gallon containers and fill them up.

We had a hut which we used as our cookhouse. Cooking was done with Calor Gas. All our crockery was plastic (courtesy of my father who worked producing these).

I enjoyed it so much that I went for 6 years in a row.

Saer Elbus
By JV

Room spinnin roon
Cannae hear a soon
Belly aa filled
Wi fear

It'll go away
I'll be okay
Gotta get oot
O this chair

Will I be wasting time
If I call 999
Hoo dae I
Get tae that phone?

This canna wait
It's probably 118
Let me hear
That ring tone

Ma heed's noo oan fire
Whit service dae yi require?
Gotta get oot
O here

Ambulance, quick
Am gonna be sick
Whit else
Dae yi need tae hear?

Leanin oan the table
Is aa that Ah'm able
Erms and legs
Dinnae work ony mare

Sweatin an freezing cauld
Makes me feel auld
Bent and dizzy
Stagger across the flaer

There'll be somebody here shin
Let paramedics in
Ful boady weight
Supported wi ma elbus

Nae time tae be nervous
Great service
It's great they're
Here tae help us

Am Ah delirious?
This is serious
Something major
Is happening here

But ma brain is still workin away
Ah can still talk and say
Ma address
And hoo tae get here

Ah wiz aw richt
Tae ah got that fricht
Is this really hoo
A big thing appears?

Whit if Ah'm wrang
An shouldnae hiv rang?
Will they think
That ah'm jist fu o fears?

Somebody's oan ma flaer
Ma elbus are aw saer
Propped up
They're aboot the only things workin

Yir in a bit o a state
It's aw richt we're no too late
We're here
Noo we'll hiv tae get movin

We'll hiv a last luk aroon
Afore we go doon
The ambulance
Is sitting there waitin

When yiv been strapped in
Then we'll begin
The journey
Ah ken yiv bin hatin

It'll no be lang noo
Yir next in the queue
The doctors
Want yi in first

Yi must feel yir in hell
But yiv din very well
Ah'm shaer
Yi'll no be the worst

A story in irregular beat to listen to and when you have done don't greet
By Stuart McIntyre

Please give me a few minutes of your time so I can tell you a story, I will warn you in advanced it does get pretty gory.

There was a young man just turned the age of 20, His life was going great but then he got thrown a curve ball or more so, plenty.

He was out celebrating his birthday when he suffered an assault, I don't know exactly what happened but the police told me it wasn't his fault.

He got smashed up pretty bad; well it was 3 on 1. Multiple skull and facial fractures but that was just some.

The worst of the damage was inside his head A severely damaged brain and rushed to hospital after being left for dead.

Society paints an unrealistic picture of how someone would be after suffering severe brain damage so I bet you anything the reality is not actually like the mental image you currently manage.

Because the man in my story wrote this poem

But my struggle goes unnoticed now and all I was trying to do at the time that night was just get home.

Emerging from a coma wasn't like the movies, I had to re-learn to walk. It was like starting life again from ground zero, I couldn't even talk

Now I look fit and healthy to every Tom Dick and Harry

But I still struggle on a daily basis and sometimes I wish I had a sign that stated that, which I could carry

With far less brain capacity there are things I can't do. Simple everyday tasks are so much harder too

So I'm forced to live with this for the rest of my days

Yes it will get better but it will always effect in many ways

Don't get me started on the justice system in this country, the assailants didn't get much punishment for what they did to me. 2 of them got let off with it and the other got 18 months in jail and after serving 4 they set him free.

But that has nothing to do with me and it's all in the past now, I just have to come to terms with the fact that when brain tissue is damaged it stays that way for good. So I'm stuck here with a life sentence on my hands that will go all the way, till I'm an old dude.

So living this has certainly taught me a thing or two or realistically many.
So do I think there is a God looking out for us up there? No there isn't any.

I do think there is more to life than just what meets the eye but having someone else in charge, calling the shots? I'm sorry that doesn't fly.

Before the injury I was working in the film industry professionally and in a short time of working I had achieved a lot.
Even though it hadn't been that long since I left a cot.

Now every day is that bit harder forever, like fighting against a strong current while swimming up a river.

I make it sound pretty bleak but there had been good things since. I did fall in love.
But my brain injury caused major problems between us and she gave me the shove.

People think I have an easy life now, but to be honest that just makes it so hard. This injury was the cause of mental health problems and if you think they are easy, you're wrong, they're off the chart.

I know I dissed god and religion but to be honest that was just to get more people talking about this and get the press.

Brain Injury is my life now so thanks for reading, I just want to raise awareness.

An Anthology
By John Campbell

An anthology is a plethora,
A concoction, a veritable
smorgasbord of a collection
Indeed a cornucopia, even
Of our creative endeavours
And a wheen a' blethers

Art

'*Skewered*' *Acrylic Painting by John Barr*

Photography by Stuart McIntyre

'*Blue Vase*' *Watercolour Painting*
by Rosemary Boyle

'Landscape' *Acrylic Painting by Graham Harkness*

'*Flowers on the Table*' *Still Life after Peploe –*
Watercolour Painting by Claire Parker

'Awe' *Watercolour Painting by John Barr*

'The Pathway' *Coloured pencil on canvas after Inam*
by Mike Gallagher

'*Autumn*' *Collage: Coloured paper, mixed twine & Card board by Karen Mitchell*

Photography by Stuart McIntyre

'White Flowers' *Acrylic Painting on canvas*
by Kirsty Lockhart

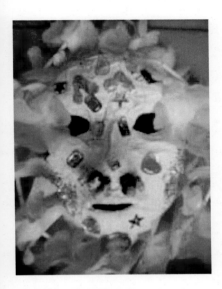

Mask by Claire Parker
Acrylic; Sequins & Tissue Paper

Mask by Steven Walker
Paper Mache; Acrylic & Pens

‘*Collage*’ *Coloured paper, glitter on card*
by Steven Walker

John Greig Dreaming
A short story by Annette Allison.

My shoulders were sore; my head was heavy and my mouth tasted like metal. I had a leaky filling. I moved my tongue across the ragged edge of one tooth. I was getting an ulcer. My eyes nipped with the lack of sleep. I had wanted it to be morning all night long. Now that it was morning, I would have given anything for an extra hour in bed. And I had some day ahead. Last week when my Dad took me and my brother to see Rangers bringing the European Cup Winners Cup back to Ibrox, I fainted. Completely flaked out. It was 1972, I was 12, and I had a lot of ground to make up. I was planning to put things right today at Station Park, when we went to see the Juniors match.

I heard my brother Jimmy open the wardrobe door in the next room and knew he was already getting set for the match. He knew nothing about my plans, mainly because he had hardly spoken to me since the fainting incident. He was ashamed and had pretty much disowned me, laughing with everyone else as the story did the rounds at school. But today, not only would he forgive me, he would be begging me to tell everybody he was my brother.

I pulled loads of clothes out of the wardrobe and had them lying on top of the bed, possible tops and bottoms together, trying to get the coolest combination. I settled on navy blue ribbed bellbottoms, a red and blue striped polo neck with a vertical rib that matched the exact width of the trouser rib. On top I knew I would be wearing my Gloverall in Airforce blue. I carefully placed the small box that would fix everything in my navy canvas duffle bag with the white pvc trim and the real rope ties.

I got through breakfast and lunch by playing with my food for that long my mother gave in and let me off with the money to buy a sausage roll and Bovril at the match. I trailed behind my brother and his pals all the way to the park. We never paid to get in. The park had corrugated metal fencing that I had only ever seen rusty and dilapidated. Silver sheets that had rotted into brown and orange and broke if you touched them. They were crumbling away on feeble worn bolts and easily swung to the side to let us in. In my head I thought the Iron Curtain looked like this. Jimmy reckoned though that what they talked about on the telly was neither iron nor a curtain. He reckoned it was a brick wall built right up the middle of Germany. Sometimes though, if you were telling him stuff, he would just say something different as if it was a fact, even if it was not, all for the sake of not letting you think you knew more than he did.

Jimmy held back one sheet for me to get through. I heard my box slide and stop against the side of the duffle bag. He looked at me. I stopped moving, still hunched down. "What's that?" he asked.

I waited a minute, trying to think what to say without giving the game away. Nothing came to mind so I just tried to pretend I had not heard him and tightened my shoelaces so he would think that was why I stopped. Then I straightened up and started to climb the banking up to the terracing. But he shouted after me, asking again. "Its private," I yelled back and picked up speed, moving down the railway sleeper steps, two at a time.

He was content to leave me at the front, at a distance he could keep an eye on me without having to get too close, and I was relieved to have got away without revealing my secret before I was ready. Standing there though, it brought back all the memories of last week. I felt myself go red and shut my eyes as the memory came creeping in. What was behind it all was me being in love with John Greig. His pictures on my brother's wall, with his beard and without, made me feel funny inside. I dreamed at night about meeting him. I dreamed during the day about how I could really make it happen. I would have been a stalker if I had the bus fares. Then, before I had time to get myself ready for it, I was close enough to touch him and it was just too much.

When Rangers beat Moscow Dynamo 3-2 in the Cup Final my Dad took us to Ibrox to see the team do a lap of honour round the Stadium on the back of a platform lorry. As they approached at a snail's pace I willed the driver to go faster until he reached us, and then to stall in front of where we were standing. We were right at the front, me and Jimmy, along with his pals and loads of other kids as the team was getting closer. I was starting to make out some of the faces and it was funny to think that all the people on Jimmy's bedroom wall were real. Colin Stein was dead easy to spot because of his blonde hair and as the lorry got nearer I could make out Derek Parlane, tall and skinny. Willie Johnstone, a hero for scoring twice in the final, looked wee and square built standing next to him. I held back from looking straight at John Greig, even though I knew exactly where he was in amongst the rest of the team, it was just too big a thing to look at his face and really see him. But at the same time as I was avoiding looking, I knew the lorry would pass soon and my chance would be gone. I kind of built up to looking at him with a sideways tackle. I started at his feet and was gradually moving upwards when someone must have passed him the cup and he lifted his arms to hold it up. I just followed where his arms were going and I saw his face a bit too quick to take it all in, to get used to the idea of seeing him and of him being real. I could hear my heart pounding as if it was right next to my ears. It felt like it was thumping in my throat and nearly choking me. I moved my tongue just so I did not choke and it touched my broken filling. At that exact moment John Greig kissed the cup. With my tongue against the filling I knew I was tasting metal the same as he was, right there and then. No one else in the park was as close to John Greig at that point. It was closer than touching him. Then I felt like I was falling, but really slowly. Everything I could see was melting together. I could not make Jimmy out from the people standing beside him. My head was light as a feather. Then it was like my legs were disappearing. I only knew they were still attached to me because I felt my knees hit the step. Then my head went backwards onto a rough bit of concrete and my face rolled onto a brown slip-on shoe.

The next thing I can remember was being in a place that smelled of disinfectant and everything echoed. There were hundreds of different kinds of glass on doors and walls that made the figures behind look dead weird. There was frosted glass with wire through it like the stuff on our front door, another kind that was ribbed and bevelled, and there was some with dimples like the panels in the top of school doors. All of it together made everything blurred and warped. The only glass you could see through was in the roof, so all I could make out was a navy blue sky. I thought I was dead.

Then I heard Jimmy tell my Dad my eyes were open. I felt his rough woollen trousers against the back of my legs and realised I was sitting on his knee. I looked up to see his face and he smiled, looking a bit relieved.

"I'm sorry, Dad," I said. He squeezed my shoulder, pulling my face in against his chest. "It was John Greig. I never thought he was real before. It was dead weird seeing him. Then I could taste the cup when he kissed it..." and I would have been out of it again if it had not been for the smell of Vosene from my hair as it fell across my face, bringing me round.

"Dad, could I not just get the bus up the road myself? I know how," Jimmy said, and then nodded in my direction. "Its dead embarrassing with her keeping flaking out like that." He sounded right fed up.

I heard his voice again now as he shook my shoulder.

"Show us what's in your bag."

I decided the moment was right. We stepped back onto an empty railway sleeper. He put down two paper cups of Bovril and pulled a white bag containing two sausage rolls out of his pocket. We both knew it was bribery but neither of us said anything. I undid the ties of my duffle bag and carefully lifted out the box frame that used to contain my sister's guide badges.

"She'll kill you," he said.

I shrugged my shoulders and carried on with the unveiling. I turned the frame face up to slowly reveal my replica Cup.

"Man, that's brilliant! Where'd you get it?" he asked.

"I made it."

He looked as if he didn't believe me and I felt my face go red with pride.

"How?" he said, as if he was going to catch me out.

"Dead easy. I cut out a picture of the real Cup from the paper, then cut round that on top of tinfoil, then I pressed down on the silver with letters from the post office set to get the imprint of the names. And then I just put plasticine at the back to keep it in place in the frame."

He fingered the outline of it through the glass. "You selling it?"

"Nah. You can have it for nothing. But you've got to say I got sent it from Ibrox because of what happened and it's a genuine replica and you can't buy them. And say it came framed. Right?" I never imagined he would like it this much.

All the time I was talking he was still looking at the Cup.

"Right?" I said again with more cheek than he would usually let me away with.

"Right," he agreed.

I knew giving it to Jimmy to show off was the surest way of living down the fainting episode.

I ran up to the hut to spend the money I skinned from the sausage roll and Bovril. You usually had to step on a milk crate to get served through the window. But I reached the window that day without using the step. I was telling my Dad about it later on. About it feeling weird. A bit like when I fainted. But he said not to worry; I was probably just levitating this time.

This is me
By Lorraine Kennedy

I am passionate about being a campaigner. I campaign on any issues which effect people with disabilities like epilepsy or mental health problems

I am also a campaigner for refugees. I think refugees have the right to have a roof over their head like everyone else and not to be thrown out onto the street.

I am against discrimination. I know how other people feel when they experience this, I have spent my whole life being discriminated against because of my learning difficulties

I'm all for a fairer society. I can get angry and bitter but I just get on and do things for other people. I'm not looking for any medals it's just the kind of person I am. I go to the groups for people with learning disabilities every other day. Sometimes you get visitors talking to you, sometimes you're active, sometimes you go out and campaign. You go out to places like George Square, handing out leaflets. You stand with banners and different speakers come up and say their piece. They come up to the front and give a speech. We don't get any hassle, maybe because people support what we've said.

There was a demo on this morning about personalisation in George Square. It usually starts about half past twelve. We sometimes go into the Council Chambers but we don't get many councillors supporting us except the ones we know. People come from all over.

We do demonstrations all over Scotland but I only manage to the Glasgow or Edinburgh ones. I go with the group and we get the train or the bus. London is too far away for me to go because I don't know my way about. I don't mind the travelling. It's not the staying there, it's that you don't know people and they don't know your ways of doing things. I'm passionate about campaigning but I won't get myself arrested. Not yet.

I feel good even if sometimes you don't think people are always listening. The crowd is listening but sometimes the people who should be listening aren't. At least you are making an effort. You're helping other people. You're not sitting moaning about it, sitting complaining, you're doing something about it even when you still may have a worry about your benefits. You are worried you'll get your benefits cut for demonstrating, it's terrible. Sometimes I take sandwiches with me. I make them at home.

I'm involved in a working group at Holyrood. I find it even harder now with the brain injury to put across what I mean because you can't think straight at times, but I keep trying.

Inglorious
By S. West

I am in my car to drive
I've drawn my map
and write my directions
and read them to go where I have to go

Now I cannot drive my car
This brain injury has pulled and put on my
handbrake
Then locked with padlock
It's taken my map and the writing,
rips it and puts it into a shredder

I get out and walk
See the road sign for Headway
Go in as they have
got the magic stick
for my gears I now need.

I try and do my art
Now I can paint my map
then go learn how to write my directions
and read what I need to do.
Now I have the golden key for my new car.

I use the gears to overtake the brain injury's
automatic van
I get my car to a parking space
that's in my own forecourt,
but I am too scared to drive it out
and feeling to call it quits.

I see in the mirrors
the brain injury van
will put me in a garage
and surround me
with a giant big wall of bricks

I look in my hands and see my angle
with the ray of life.
Tell me that Headway is here
with the petrol station of life.

I get the set of headlights
for my car to see through
the brain injury's darkness
of their own lust for life

Now I can drive my car
on my map
and read my own directions
and go to the road bridge
to the new land to
grow my life.

Something about St. Valentine
By Sean Riach

Did he have his head chopped off?
Spilling red ink like a burst biro
Gushing with brutal praise
His anatomical heart
Frantically fulfilling
It's temporal liberty from the mind

Or was it poison?
Just like Galileo
The old asp defanged
In a horrible choice
We'll stove in your brilliance
Wi this here blunt force
Trauma device.
It'll smash into the centre
Of yur Universe.
No like it? Drink
This here vile vale

O secret stuff.
Put it to your lips
Like a kiss wi an adder
Tot up the pros and cons
Slovenly slurp this
Absence of love
Feel it pickle yir blud
Bud let yur heart
Turn to stone'

Balanced Pools
BY JV

Life on this Earth
Can be Heaven or Hell
By Birth
Or feeling unwell

Carrying loads
Covered in muck
Slimy hilly roads
Run out of luck

Busy in groups
All alone
Out with the troops
Too broken to moan

Posture perfect
Built up with hay
Keep your own respect
Relief at the end of the day

Fishermen
Bobbing the seas
Children
With families to please

Bundle of bricks
On the head
Pile of sticks
Just to be fed

Rice fields
Like balanced pools
Water over heels
Following natures rules

Across under the waterfall
Remembering the price
Fumbling along the wall
Tied together on the ice

Mountain top town
Green valley below
Soaring eagle looking down
Face all aglow

Cry Freedom
By Rosemary Boyle

What does freedom mean to me? It means freedom to express oneself

Freedom from the constraints given to the people

Freedom of expression

Cry freedom

Freedom of a political system that gags so many of us

Freedom to be who we truly are and not what we are told to be

The political elite always dictating to the population, it's like the old saying "do as I say, but don't do as I do"

What freedom will we have in the future? The way things are going, very little

Alas, let's analyse and look at what's expected of us today

We are gagged, you cannot speak your mind otherwise you are jailed

The political elite creating new laws to imprison us. They say we have free speech, but when we use that right, they throw the book at us.

Politicians say they speak the **TRUTH,** but all they do is speak in a language to confuse the common man and woman, deliberately to gain votes.

A Flight
By S. West

The view below is the time

Leave the ground and flow through the air

Now go slow, the soft sound is heard

Below is the place outside

My Dream
By S. West

The picture you see, has the thoughts

Yes feel what you feel

And see what you see

Light and dark make the shades

The face you see and can have

It's where the past will rest

Travelling Hopefully
By Mark Osborne

Petrol in my tank

Pink Floyd on my player

Oh, Rotterdam and Amsterdam

Through both I did roam

But now – Troon's my destination

Though Largs caused a minute's hesitation

It'll be a seafront saunter

And a pie supper feast

And dodging the muck

Of the big, flying,

recycling beast

Doon the water
By Mike Gallagher

There was a wee man from Dunoon

Who went up in the air haudin a balloon

He met an old bird

He said "this is absurd"

Tell me? How am I gaunae to get Doon

Smell the Lunches
By JV

Arrive in the car park
Surrounded by huge trees
Inhabited by crows
Calling to each other

No wind gets in
It's peaceful and calm
Slight rustling of leaves
The sound of golf shoes

Walk past the old hotel
Smell the lunches being cooked
Children laughing and running
Along the huge expanse of grass

Rhododendron bushes and trees
In full bloom
Dozens of different birds
Singing in the sunshine

Families picnicking
Arran away in the distance
Across the blue, blue sea
Smell the salty sea air

Pudding Poem
By John Campbell

Sticky Toffee Pudding

With custard to coincide

Toffee Pecan Roulade

Raspberry Roulade by my side

Strawberry Sponge Cake

Muller Yoghurt

Morning, evening, any time of the day

Raspberry Pavlova

Crème Brulée

Crème Caramel

Rice Pudding

I devour them all

And refuse nothing but blows

Hot day at Headway
By John Campbell

On a hot day at Headway

There's nothing I like better than a seat in the Sydney Devine

Atop the Stewart McCall

Providing it's not too Bertie Auld

And I do enjoy the extremely palatable biscuits

But never like to be too Aiden McGeady

Poem about my cat Lucy Claire Paton
By Vivien Claire Paton and Tom Paton

I have a little cat and her name is Lucy Claire.
She has lovely yellow eyes, and shiny thick black
hair.

As she is a house cat, she is not allowed outdoors.

But she enjoys her many fluffy toys and chases
them round the floors.

She is really a lovely friend to me and always
brightens my days.

So I wish that the joy she always brings, with me
forever stays.

My cat is depressed
By DT

My cat is depressed
He just sits about
Not eating his dinner
And not going out

He ignores his toy mouse
And his feathers on a string
He ignores me too
He ignores everything

So if you know a cure
For depression in pets
Then please help him out
As he doesn't trust vets

The Cows are Out!
By Pandora

It was a dark and windy night. It was late March and it was lambing season. I was working on a farm and I had volunteered myself to do my stint on nightshift first. There were two of us helping the farmers with the lambing this year and from previous experience I had found that getting nightshift over with first was the easier option.

There were almost three hundred pregnant ewes left to lamb. Any one of them could lamb at any time. They were a mixture of Blackfaces, Texels and Suffolks and if a ewe looked like she was going to lamb I had to go into the pen, catch her and take her into a lambing pen. Catching the ewe was easier said than done, especially if she was a blackface. The blackfaces are a small, hardy breed of sheep well suited to the Scottish hills. They are incredibly nimble and if they don't want to be caught it can be a long process to catch them. However, they do have these useful things called horns and if you can get standing abreast of the ewe it is possible to drag and steer her into a lambing pen.

The sheep were split between ten different pens. I had been around the pens observing them and no-one looked as if she might be ready to lamb at any time soon. I had fifteen clean lambing pens ready for when a ewe was ready for one. Six of them were occupied with ewes and lambs looking quite content. They had all been fed and watered and all mothers had plenty of milk for their twin lambs. There were a few pet lambs that were asleep in a heap in the pet box under a heat lamp. I had fed them earlier from a bottle so they were happy. I had to be careful when feeding the pets because they would guzzle away till they blew up like wee balloons and that wasn't good for them. Pets were usually the weakest from a set of triplets. It was unusual for a ewe that had given birth to triplets to be allowed to go out to grass with all three. She probably wouldn't have had enough milk to be able to rear three healthy lambs. There was one tiny lamb in the warming box. It had been the smallest of a set of triplets and I'd given it it's last dose of colostrum. It was getting stronger all the time so would be joining the other pets soon.

I decided to take a wander round the sheep pens then clean out the lambing box making sure everything I needed to assist a ewe to give birth was there. I had learned the things to look out for in previous years. A ewe getting close to lambing would appear to be restless and as her lambing time approached she would start making a bed for herself in the pen. It could often be quite difficult to know which ewe to go to first and I had seen me get several ewes into their lambing pens and then gone to lamb them literally one after the other in quick succession.

I absolutely loved my time working on the farm. I could forget about all my worries back home. The only thing that mattered for that time was the lambing. A few odd moments when I was left alone doing nightshift there might be a worrying time but just now it was relatively peaceful, considering all that was going on with the lambing.

Still nobody looked like she was going to lamb soon so I busied myself tidying up. I swept up around the lambing pens and the pet box, washed out the baby bottles that I'd used to feed the pets and checked on all the ewes and lambs that were in the lambing pens. All was quiet.

It was a beautiful night apart from the howling wind. I loved those nights in the countryside where it's properly dark and the stars are so visible and it's just me and the sheep. I thought I might go and lie in the straw shed and look up at the stars. My worry was always that I might end up dozing off to sleep. It took a while for my body clock to adjust to the nightshift. One more check around the sheep first. All still quiet.

As I turned to head out to the straw shed I saw something moving. I did a double take. It couldn't be. It was. The farmers' entire herd of prize winning Limousin cattle were on the move outside. It was coming up to their calving season but I wasn't involved in that. I didn't know if the farm road gate was shut. If it wasn't there could be a disaster. There was no time to run down to check. Without hesitation I raced up to the farmhouse, raced up the stairs and knocked loudly on the farmers' bedroom door. "Quick! The cows are out and I don't know if the gate is shut!" I ran back outside, the farmers and their eleven year old son following fast behind me.

The farm gate had not been shut and ten or so cows were fast making their way across to the small village directly opposite the farm. The villagers had very neat and tidy front gardens which they obviously took great pride in. Flower beds were well attended to and lawns were neatly mown. By the time we caught up with the cows several of them were wreaking havoc in the gardens and villagers were appearing in their nightclothes to see what on earth was going on.

I stayed by the roadside and signalled to any traffic to slow down. Some cattle were heading off down the road so first I had to run to get ahead of them and turn them around. The farmers' son thought the whole thing was brilliant. I don't think there had been this much excitement on the farm for a long time. The farmers themselves were less impressed.

How we managed it I'll never know but together we managed to get the cattle rounded up, back up the farm road and back into their pens. All the time we were doing this joint effort I couldn't help but worry about the sheep I'd left. Once it was all over I ran quickly round all of the sheep pens. Thankfully nobody had decided to lamb while I was away. Phew!

The three of them went back to bed, but not for long. It was nearly breakfast time.

As for my lambing assistant friend, she slept peacefully throughout this whole fiasco. Exhausted from a hard day's farming, I imagine.

I don't know whether the farmers ever made friends with the villagers again and I don't know if we'll ever know how the cows got out in the first place. Was it anybody's fault? Who knows?

My Favourite Place 2
By Innes Walker

A place I really love is the small village of Lamlash on the Isle of Arran. The first sight of Arran comes from the Cal-mac ferry, approaching Brodick Bay. From the Bay you can clearly see the Holy Isle which lies just off the coast of Lamlash.

When I get off the ferry, there is always a strong smell of fish and chips from the Pier Chip Shop, and the clacking of seagulls circling overhead hoping to be thrown a few chips.

I have had a fish supper from that very chip shop and the fish tastes fantastic, maybe because it's been freshly caught from one of the trawlers, red, blue and green, that bob up and down in the harbour.

After getting off the ferry the next stage of the journey involves boarding one of the buses which are lined up ready to take passengers to the various villages around the island. I board the Lamlash one.

After boarding, I find a nice comfortable seat, hopefully next to the windows in order to get a view of the stunning landscapes on the short journey. Up the hill, then looking down onto one of the best views anywhere – over the bay of Lamlash onto the Holy Isle which is now a spiritual retreat run by Buddhists. A place of peace.

They are gone 2
By Margaret Thomson

They're deid
They're deid
They used to be in my heid
But ever since the bleed
They're deid

Rosemary Boyle Cry Freedom, For the Love of a Son or Daughter, Watercolour "Blue Vase"; all©2012 R.Boyle

J V Smell the Lunches, Balanced Pools, Saer Elbus. all©2012 J. Vincent;

S. West 'Collage' with coloured paper, Inglorius, A Flight, My Dream, Mask; all ©2012 S. Walker

John Campbell An Anthology, Pudding Poem, Hot day at Headway; all ©2012 J.Campbell;

Leo Mushet Poem for Elizabeth ©2012 L.Mushett

Mark Osborne Travelling Hopefully ©2012 M Osborne

Vivien Paton and Tom Paton Poem about my cat Lucy ©2012 V.Paton ;

D T My Cat is depressed ©2012 D.Thomson

Margaret Thomson A refuge, They are gone 1,They are gone 2; all ©2012 M.Thomson

Lorraine Kennedy This is me, My favourite place 3; all ©2012 L.Kennedy;

Michael Gallacher It's hard to write a poem, Doon the water, Coloured pencil on canvas 'The Pathway'; all ©2012 M. Gallacher

Annette Allison John Greig Dreaming ©2012 A.Allison ;

Bob Colquhuon My favourite place 1 ©2012 B.Colquhoun ;

Innes Walker My favourite place 2 ©2012 I.Walker ;

Pandora The Cows are Out ©2012 P.Watt;

Stuart McIntyre A story in irregular beat, Photographs 1 & 2; Front Cover photograph all ©2012 S.McIntyre;

Sean Riach About an Auntie, Something about St. Valentine; all ©2012 S.Cumming;

Looby Loo Travelling Light ©2012 L. McAndrew;

Jane McQueen Going on a Steam Train ©2012 J.McQueen ;

Neill Sloan Cycles ©2012 N.Sloan ;

John Barr Painting 1 Acrylic Painting 'Skewered', Watercolour Painting 'Awe'; all ©2012 J.Barr ;

Karen Mitchell Collage 'Autumn' ©2012 K.Mitchell ;

Claire Parker Still life Watercolour 'Flowers on the table', Mask; all ©2012 C.Parker;

Graham Harkness 'Landscape' in Acrylic ©2012 G.Harkness;

Kirsty Lockhart 'White Flowers' Acrylic ©2012 K.Lockhart